Again, David's Having Distractions

Friggin Chicken

Teresa Oliver

Published By:
Teresa Oliver
misstoliver@comcast.net

Designed & Produced by:
Custom Made For You
graphic design & printing studio
(770) 923-8783
www.custommadeforyou.net

Edited by
Michael Oliver
Teresa Oliver
Gloria Whitehead
Jaffe Hendricks

Dedication

Again, David's Having Distractions is dedicated to the parents, teachers, and other individuals who interact with a child with ADHD (or any other mental or physical disability). Often times, these individuals are misunderstood because of their unique behavior and learning profiles; causing them to feel awkward and alone. Society has done a great job at accepting typically developing students, but has not done a great job of accepting the those who do not fit the typical mold. Instead of celebrating the natural diversity inherent in human brains, too often we medicalize and pathologize the diversity in human brains (Armstrong, 2010). Which could potentially stifle the growth and the creative abilities in these young minds. We need to admit that there is no standard cultural or racial group, and that in fact, diversity among brains is just as wonderfully enriching as biodiversity and the diversity among cultures and races (Armstrong, 2010).

In David's case, daydreaming has gotten a bad reputation, and his thoughts have often got him yelled at and misunderstood. However, daydreamers are often the people that make things happen. They are creative and motivated even when it appears they are not. I dare everyone who reads this book to dream- daydream. Dream the biggest most ridiculous dream. Then take the first step, and make it happen.

Academia is a collection of books that is geared towards increasing the vocabulary and literary skills in young readers. It contains and expounds on concepts like figurative language and inference which helps reinforce reading skills that are taught inside the classroom. Along with reinforcing literacy skills, these books are designed to encourage independence and a love of reading.

Chapter 1
Introduction

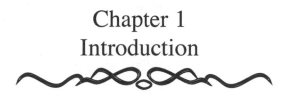

Okay.
So I finally made it to the fourth grade, and boy has this journey been rough. First, let me tell you guys a little bit about myself. My name is David Allen and I hate school! Ever since I started this school business, my life has been **horrendous**- absolutely **mind boggling**.

Let me go back to where it all began- the first grade.
The teachers in the first grade were just like prison guards. It's always sit down this, pay attention that, don't touch this *aaaaaand* they even stopped having snack time. And, it was in this grade that I began to notice that I was different from other kids.

See, I'm one of the shortest guys in class. I'm kind of skinny, which makes my clothes sort of baggy. Plus, I have this really weird hair. It looks kind of like a cross between a skunk and a porcupine. None of the other kids in my class seem to have any of these problems.

Take this kid Michael Hunter, for example. He has the best hair, the best clothes; he's the best at everything. He always gets first place, ALWAYS! This year's spelling bee, he won the biggest trophy. I think he secretly bribed the judges because they gave him all the easy words and gave me all hard words. When we got our report cards he made all A's, and when we play outside games for P.E., he always wins! Me, on the other hand, I'm never first at anything. Sometimes, I'm even last. Can you believe that? LAST!

---

horrendous (hor-ren-dous). adj.-terrible
mind boggling (mind bog-gling). adj.-overwhelming; startling

The other kids in my class seem to be able to sit still and focus, but not me. I'm always moving, fidgeting, and trying to focus on my teacher. She says I have ants in my pants. I say she's *sooo* unbelievably boring that I have to move and squirm to keep my buns from falling asleep.

At home, things are no different. Instead of my family's last name being Allen, the family's name should be the Perfects minus David. See, my mother is president of one of the biggest companies in Illinois; my dad is an Illinois state court judge- clearly two jobs that require perfection from me. Heaven forbid I would ever do anything to embarass them.

My older sister, Emma, does everything right according to my parents. She's in the sixth grade, and she thinks she's hot stuff. *With her perfect dresses and her perfect pigtails. Little Miss Perfect!* NOT!! Little Miss Suck Up is more like it. Room always clean. Homework always complete. *Neh, neh, neh.*

I'm starting to think she and Michael Hunter are related. Oh, and don't even get me started on my younger brother Aaden. He's six months old and *soooooo* cute. Once again- another phrase from my parents. I don't see what's so cute about him. He's fat, bald, and he even drools! So here I am son of Mr. and Mrs. Do Everything Right and stuck in between little Miss Perfect and Mr. Soooooo Cute.

Chapter 2
The Perfects

"Daaavid."

"DAAaaavid."

"DAVID!!"

"Yes mom."

"Didn't you hear me calling you?"

"Nooo. If I heard you, I would have answered you," I mumbled under my breath.

"What did you say David?"

"Huh?! Oh ummm-- nothing Mom." Boy, she has ears like a bat I thought to myself.

"Your sister and brother are almost done eating breakfast and you haven't even started. Hurry up before you make us late again!" she said in a very **aggravated** voice.

"Yeah, hurry up slow poke before you make us late," shouted Emma.

"MOM!," I yelled.

---

aggravated (ag-gra-vat-ed). adj. – to rouse to exasperation or anger; to make worse, more serious, or more severe

"Emma, leave your brother alone please," Mom said calmly.

"But mom he's always..."

"No buts, Emma. David, just hurry up please," Mom said again sounding very aggravated.

I wonder why every time mom talks to me she sounds aggravated and annoyed, but Little Miss Priss gets the calm voice. And how does Mom think I, me, King David makes everyone late.

"David Allen!"

"Huh. I mean, yes sir," I said startled.

"Are you day dreaming again?!" Dad asked.

Now he's annoyed. Geesh, I thought to myself.

"No. I was just thinking that Mom..."

Dad rudely interrupted, "Did you hear what your mother said?"

"Yes, dad."

"Well hurry up then! Stop day dreaming and get a move on."

"But I wasn't day dreaming!"

"NO BUTS MISTER."

"And did you remember to put your homework in your book bag?"

"Well, uhhh, actually, I can't exactly *find* my homework."

"David Allen, how many times do I have to tell you after you finish your homework to put it in your book bag right away?"

"Dad, I was about to put it up when Aaden came in and drooled and slobbered all over my video games."

"So are you trying to tell me that these video games are more important than putting your homework away?"

"No Dad. I'm just saying..."

"Well then, hush up! Find your homework or there will be NO video games for the rest of the week," said Dad while walking out of my room.

"Well then, hush up or there will be no video blah blah blah."

"David! What did you say young man?"

"Huh?! Oh. Umm nothing Dad."

Again, David's Having Distractions
Page 10

Chapter 3
Slam Dunk You

7:43 am. Two minutes until the bell rings and two minutes until Mrs. Morris will take attendance. I cannot be tardy today. Today is the most important day of my life. The class gets to pick what we want to do for Fall Festival. And, if I'm late, then I will have to go to the office to get a tardy slip and there will be only sucky choices left.

Ding. Ding. Ding. DONG!

Whew! 7:45. Made it just in time.

"Alright class! Settle down, settle down. Everyone, please take your seat," said Mrs. Morris. "Now that David's here we can finally get started. Everyone knows what today is, right?" asked Mrs. Morris as she looked at the class through her square glasses that rested on the end of her pointy nose.

"YES," the class answered all together.

"And you all know that I want each and every one of you to represent our class as the best fourth grade at Dublin Elementary, right?"

"YES," the class answered again in **unison**.

"Okay. So, let's get started!" This time we are going to do things a little different. Instead of picking activities from the board, this time we are going to pick activities by playing the fastest draw.

---

unison (u-ni-son). n. – at the same time, all at once, all together

"Yeaaa!!" yelled the class.

Nooooo, I thought to myself as I slumped down in my seat. See, every class in the entire school is celebrating fall by having a Fall Festival. Each class gets to choose activities for all the students to participate in, and the class that has the best activities gets to have a field trip day. Last year, the 5th graders had the best activities, and Mr. Hall's class won. They got to go to downtown Chicago and have pizza and hot dogs. The student in the class who has the best game gets a homework pass for one week and student of the month. The winner last year was Corey Hunter, Michael Hunter's brother- need I say more.

Whoever wins this year will get to go to Great America! Great America has the biggest and fastest roller coasters of all the amusement parks I've ever been to. They also have cotton candy, hamburgers, pizza, french fries, snow cones, and...

"DAVID!," yelled Mrs. Morris. "Are you day dreaming again?"

"No ma'am. I was just..."

"Yes, I know- you were just distracted by all those silly thoughts in your head. Now I was just telling the class that we are going to play fastest draw to decide which game each student will be doing. I have written the games on the board and whoever is the fastest draw will win until all the games are gone. The class has a choice between 12 games. Some games can be administered with only one person; other games may require two or more people to facilitate the game. This year the fourth grade choices are: Crazy Eights, Slam Dunk You, Webble Wobble, Hats Off, Long Ranger, Hop Scotch, Dos and Don'ts, Guess This, Don't Fall, Spin and Sit, and last but not least Friggin Chicken."

Duh, I thought to myself. That was so **redundant**. Every year each grade has the same games.

"David's game is going to be Friggin Chicken because he looks like baked chicken," yelled a boy in the back of the class.

"No his hair looks like chickens have been pecking at it. That's why he needs to get Friggin Chicken," said Ashley who was sitting in the front row.

The entire class laughed as I sat there with smoke coming from my ears, but I knew if I said anything in **retaliation** I might really be stuck with that ole dumb Friggin Chicken game.

"Okay class that's enough. Ashley and Joey you are not allowed to have recess today. That's considered bullying, and it simply won't be tolerated. Now as I was saying, everyone knows how this game works--- I will call on two students and give you a math or reading question. Whoever raises their hand first and can answer the question correctly is the fastest draw."

---

redundant (re-dun-dant). adj. —not or no longer needed or useful; repetitive in expression
retaliation (re-tal-i-a-tion). v. – to return like for like, especially evil for evil

I hate this game! I never get to be the fastest draw and she always makes me and Michael Hunter compete against each other.

"Okay class it's game time! First up, are the girls."
"Katie and Megan come on down. Question one: what's the square root of 81?" Mrs. Morris said in her lame game show voice.

Katie's hand flew up first.

"Uh, uh, umm seven," she answered.

"Eh, wrong answer," Mrs. Morris replied- still talking in her game show voice. "Megan if you know the correct answer you can have first pick."

"The answer is nine. Nine times nine equals 81."

"Good job Megan. You have first pick."

"Please don't pick Slam Dunk You... please don't pick Slam Dunk You," I said quietly to myself.

"I want my game to be that one," she said as she pointed towards the board.

"Which one Megan dear?" Mrs. Morris said.

"The first one… Crazy Eights."

Whew. That was close. I thought for sure she would have chosen Slam Dunk You- Everyone loves that game!

"Next up are the boys. Let's have David Allen..."

Please not Michael Hunter. Please not Michael Hunter.

"...And Michael Hunter," STILL in her game show voice.

Ugh, I knew it. It's always me against him, Mr. First Place. Both of us will want the same game, Slam Dunk You. This game always has a line a mile long, and is **notorious** for winning at Fall Festival. If I want to be the winner, I have to have Slam Dunk You.

As we were waiting for the teacher to find a question, we both had our games faces on ready to **devour** each other if necessary. We both wanted the same pick and this time Michael wasn't going to beat me!

"Okay you two—your question is going to be an English question. What is a compound sentence?"

Michael's and my hand leaped from our laps at the same time.

"Oh, we have a tie. Both hands were up at the same time. So, now you guys have to guess a number that I am thinking of, whoever is the closest to that number wins."

She whispered the number to Ashley.

"Michael?"
"I pick number one because I am number one," he said as he glared at me.

"Your turn David."

"I pick number five," I said while clenching my jaw.

"The winner is Michael!"

"The number that I was thinking of was number two."

---

notorious (no-to-ri-ous) . adj. – famous or well known, typically for some bad quality or deed
devour (de-vour). v. – eat hungrily or quickly; to destroy, consume, or waste

"CHEATERS!" I screamed.

"Michael always picks number one and we ALL know that. This isn't fair. I want a rematch. CHEATERS, CHEATERS, CHEATERS!" I chanted.

"MISTER ALLEN!! Stop it! If you continue to blurt out such nonsense, then I will completely remove you from the game and from Fall Festival."

"This is so unfair. It's **unjust**. It's highway robbery. It's Ceasar and Brutus. It's..."

"David, zip your lips before you have a one way ticket to the principal's office. Now, if you don't mind- let's continue everyone. If that's okay with you Mr. Allen?"

"Yes, we can continue," I replied feeling very defeated.

"Michael if you know the answer you have second pick."

"A compound sentence is two simple sentences put together with a conjunction."

"Wonderful Michael! That's absolutely positively correct!"

"Wait a minute," I said. "A compound sentence? Really? A compound sentence? That's something we learned in the second grade. You ALWAYS GIVE HIM THE EASY QUESTIONS!"

"Calm down David. The question could have easily been given to either one of you," she said sternly.

"Gimme a break," I yelled. "You know Michael is faster than me,

---

unjust (un-just). adj. – unfair

you know he always picks the number one and YOU know that I'm right. Now that I have uncovered you guys' sinister plan, I should have second pick."

"Surely, you don't really believe all that rubbish you are blurting out?"

"Yes. I believe it and it is true! IT'S TRUE! Cheaters, I tell ya. Cheaters."

"Alright David, I have had enough. *Eeeenough!* Out of my classroom and straight to the principal's office you go!"

"But wait, if I go to the office, I won't get a chance to pick a game, and I won't be ..."

"No buts David! OUT!"

Again, David's Having Distractions

Chapter 4
The Principal's Office

"Good morning, Mrs. Johnson." Mrs. Johnson is the school's secretary. She has been at Dublin for as long as I've been alive. She looks like she's about four feet tall. She has the whitest of white hair, and her skin is all wrinkly and droopy. I'm not sure how old she is but it's a rumor going around that she's as old as the first **prehistoric** dinosaurs. If my calculations are correct that's about a trazillion years old

"Good morning, David. Sent to the principal's office again I see?"

"Yeah, but this time it wasn't my fault. Mrs. Morris and Michael plotted a secret sinister plan that added to my **demise**. Let me tell you about it Mrs. Johnson."

"Yeah, but nothing," she said sternly interrupting me. "It's never your fault, is it David?" she said glaring at me. "Straight into Dr. Jackson now young man," as she pointed down the long dark **drab** hallway.

Knock. Knock. Knock.

"Come in. Ah, David back so soon? Weren't you just here yesterday afternoon?"

"Yes sir, Dr. Jackson. I'm back."

---

prehistoric (pre-his-tor-ic). adj. – the period before written records; outdated
demise (de-mise). n. – the end of existence or activity; termination
drab (drab). adj. – lacking brightness or interest; drearily dull

"What happened *this* time, David? Although I'm sure it's not your fault," he said sarcastically.

"Mrs. Morris is so mean and she hates me, and she loves Michael Hunter."

"Oh really?" said the principal, but I couldn't decide if his tone was sarcastic or annoyed.

"Yeah, really she *looooves* him. Like I think she wants to like marry him and be in love kissy face with him."

"Alright David one more inappropriate comment like that and you will be suspended for 3 days! Now tell me what really happened, and try to stick to the facts and keep your personal opinion out of it!"

"The story is going to make me look like I lost my cool or acted uhh—uhh—what's the word my mom always using? Is it im-bracive, imrational, impulsate?"

"Impulsive. David, **impulsive**. The word is impulsive."

"Yes, Dr. Jackson! That's it… impulsive."

"Well young man, we have had this talk before. You need to get control of your behavior and outbursts. No one likes a kid who constantly disrupts and blurts out in class. Now, I want you to sit here for 20 minutes and calm down. When you return to class I want you to apologize to your teacher and classmates."

I can't stay here for 20 minutes. I will miss the rest of the game and my chances at picking Slam Dunk You, I said to myself. What can I do? Think fast, think fast! Got it! Maybe I could drool a little

---

impulsive (im-pul-sive). adj. – acting or done without forethought

and give the super sad face. It always seems to work for my sister and brother.

"Dr. Jackson please don't make me stay in here for 20 minutes. I will miss a great lesson that Mrs. Morris is teaching all the other students," I said, trying to sound as sincere as I possibly could. Like Emma does when she gets in trouble. I even managed to drool a little like Aaden, all the while having sad puppy dog eyes, and a pouty face.

"David! Stop your silly **antics**! Stop that very unconvincing face and please stop that drooling.

Take this tissue, wipe your mouth, and go sit in the front with Mrs. Johnson until you have calmed yourself or I'm calling your parents."

"Yes sir."

---

antics (an-tics). n. – foolish, outrageous, or amusing behavior

Chapter 5
Friggin Chicken

Eighteen minutes down. That means I have 120 seconds left in my 20 minute time out or as I would like to call it—my death sentence. It wasn't so bad though. Mrs. Johnson had managed to keep herself busy and away from her desk, which meant away from me.

Clock still ticking; countdown begins. 1 Mississippi, 2 Mississippi, 3 Mississippi- I forget why some people count and say Mississippi in between but it doesn't matter because really soon King David will be back in the class and ready to take over the world.

Minute 19... Only 60 seconds left. Time to start the count down 60... 59... 58... 57... 56 ...

"Hello Wimp!" Michael Hunter said with an ugly smirk on his face.

55... 54...Just ignore him I thought to myself.

"I SAID hello wimp! So the loser boy can't hear now. Well, since you're so deaf it won't bother you if I say this: You and your entire family are losers. You smell like dog's butt and no one likes you."

48... 47... I'm still counting down and trying my best to ignore him.

"You suck at sports, your clothes are too big and your hair looks so dumb."

32... 31... 30...

"And did I mention that the only game left for Fall Festival is Friggin Chicken," Michael said while laughing. "HAHA Friggin Chicken! Because you're a piece of fried chicken sandwich."

"That's it!" I yelled. "I can't take it anymore." I leaped out of my chair and tried to tackle him! Wham! But somehow I ended up on the floor, and took Mrs. Johnson's office phone with me.

"David and Michael!" yelled Mrs. Johnson. "What is going on in here? What are you doing? Get up and pick up that phone."

"Oh! Mrs. Johnson I'm so glad you came in. David just tried to attack me for no reason. He leaped over the table and knocked over the phone too. Luckily, I was swift on my feet and he hit the floor instead of me," he said **slyly**. "I was just standing here minding my own bees wax and he tried to clobber me for no reason. He's an animal- pure animal I tell ya."

"Mister Allen, we are tired of your foolishness and your disruptions."

"Mrs. Johnson! He's lying and you're falling for it. Why would I, the smallest kid in our class, attack the biggest kid in our class? Let's use our brains here!"

"Are you saying I'm not using my brain, Mr. Allen?"

"Yes. I mean no. Well – ummm sorta."

---

slyly (sly-ly). adj. – clever or cunning

"See David Allen is an animal. He attacked me and now he is saying you don't have a brain."
"Straight in to Dr. Jackson's office David. I'm going to let you explain how you behaved and this time you are really going to get it" scolded Mrs. Johnson.

"Twice in one day---he should be caged like a zoo animal," I heard Michael tell Mrs. Johnson as I took baby steps towards Dr. Jackson's office.

Maybe if I walk extremely slow the bell will ring and it will be time to go home. Or I could hide in the supply closet and everyone will think zombies ate me and will forget about all the trouble that

Friggin Chicken
Page 25

I'm in.

THE SUPPLY CLOSET!! That's it! I'm a genius!

It's right here! Right next to the lost and found, and the door is unlocked!

Oooo and it's just enough room for me right here between the paper mache stuff and last year's Christmas play costumes. First, I better lock the door so no one can get in.

Boy it sure is dark in here, but I'm not afraid, I said aloud to myself while looking for a comfy spot. I will just wait here until its time to go home.

This will be King David's magical disappearing act. All of them will be so sorry they were ever mean to me. They will be so sorry that they will want to serve the king and bring him presents. That Michael Hunter will be the king's jester, and his outfit will be pink and purple with gold medallions on the hat. The entire class will laugh at him, his funny clothes, and stupid hat. Just wait and see.

Chapter 6
Big Trouble

Clickitty. Click. Click. (keys turning in the lock)

Oh no. Someone is trying to open the door. Maybe I can pretend to be a statue or I can curl up like one of these balls.

Oh no! Please don't see me. Please don't see me.

"David? Is that you? What are you doing in the supply closet? And why are you standing there like the Statue of Liberty? Come out of there right now young man!" demanded Mrs. Morris.

I stood there with a blank stare because I didn't know how to respond.

"David, answer me immediately! What in the world were you doing hiding in the supply closet in the dark?"

I opened my mouth, and tried to speak but no words would come out for several seconds. Then, finally I said," Please don't tell Dr. Jackson, please don't tell Mrs. Johnson, and please whatever you do don't tell my parents!" I said while sobbing.

"You still haven't told me what you're doing in here David, and **apparently** you've been in here since earlier. Its only twenty minutes before the dismissal bell rings. Have you been in here all day?" she asked. I'm sorry but I'm going to have to tell your parent about this."

---

apparently (ap-par-ent-ly). adv. – as far as one knows or can see

I cried harder and begged for mercy. "Please, please, please Mrs. Morris. I will tell you what happened."

After taking a few minutes to explain what happened between Michael and me, I waited to hear what Mrs. Morris was going to do. Was she going to tell my parents and Dr. Jackson?

"David."

"Yes, Mrs. Morris?"

"You behaved so poorly because of a fall festival game? You accused me of cheating. You said I loved Michael. You told Mrs. Johnson she didn't have a brain. You tried to attack your classmate, and hid in a supply closet all day, simply because you wanted the game Slam Dunk You?"

"Yes ma'am," I said.

"Follow me back to the class."

Ding. Ding. Ding. DONG.

The dismissal bell rang loud and clear as we began walking back to the classroom. All the students were going to the bus lanes, the car riders' lane, or the after school program. But not me. I, King David, was walking back to the classroom to get **beheaded**. As we got closer to the classroom, I began to imagine me having super human power. I would freeze time and create a secret underground tunnel. In the tunnel, I would be able to control all the punishments that parents and teachers could give kids like me. Kids who are smart but everyone thinks are dumb. Kids who move fast but everyone thinks move slow. Kids who have to deal with other kids like Michael Hunter. Our punishment would be pizza parties, video

---

beheaded (be-head). v. – cut off the head of someone

games, and no school. All the other kids would have to do algebra and eat the tuna noodle surprise that they serve in the lunchroom every Wednesday. All the teachers would have to give us chips, candies, and a dessert buffet of all kinds. That would be the best punishment and I would be number one not that Michael Hunter.

"Uh hem," Mrs. Morris said to get my attention. "Again, David you are having those distractions aren't you? I wonder what's so amazing in that head of yours. I have been looking at you for almost 45 seconds and you have just stood there gazing into space. Whatever it is you're thinking about please try to control it while I talk to you. Now, I brought you back to the class so I could give you all the game pieces for Friggin Chicken. At first, I thought the best punishment would be to remove you from Fall Festival completely, but after hearing you whine about the game you didn't get, I thought making you host Friggin Chicken would be better."

Then suddenly the intercom inturrupted. *Beep* *The school intercom came on: David Allen to the front. Your ride is waiting- David Allen to the front... your ride is waiting. *Beep**

I stood up headed towards the door thinking I had managed to escape my sentencing, but I was wrong.

"No, no, not just yet. I'm not finished young man. Don't you even want to know why I'm going to make you host that game?"

"Not really" I said as I plopped back in my seat.

"Well, I'm going to tell you anyway. You were being such a sore loser and showed such poor sportsmanship that I thought I should allow you the chance to change your attitude. And have an opportunity to win best game show host at Fall Festival. Does that right sound like the right thing to do?"

"Not really" I said as I placed my hands on my face.

Beep Second call... David Allen to the front. David Allen to the front. Your ride is waiting. *Beep*

"It sounds like I have the lamest game in the whole entire world and I'm not going to win. No one ever wants to play Friggin Chicken. It's the dumbest game ever. Who even invented this game? Who thought to tie a rope around a chicken and fling it in the air? Chickens don't fly in real life anyway. So the game doesn't even make sense."

"I understand your concerns David, but remember this is your game and you can be as creative as you want. You have thousands of thoughts and a great imagination; use your creativity to make this game awesome. Make it the best game in the entire school."

"But how can I do that?"
"Just use your imagination and believe in yourself. Now get your book bag and the supplies for the game so you can go home."
"Alright," I said as we walked up the hallway. "Mrs. Morris can I ask you a question?"
"Yes, David?"
"Are you still going to tell my parents about today?"
"Yes. Your conduct was very unsatisfactory today, but I will ask them to take it easy on you."
"Thanks."

Again, David's Having Distractions

Chapter 7
Silence Isn't Always Golden

"Why are you always the last child to come out of the school? What happened this time? Did you forget your book bag again? Did you forget what you have to do for homework? Look at you – tie your shoes and tuck your shirt in."

My mom always wanted me to look nice and neat like the rest of the Perfects. I can't wait until I turn 13. I'm never cleaning my room, tucking my shirt in, or tying my shoes. I won't have to follow any rules because I will be a teenager.

"Good afternoon Mrs. Allen. Can I speak with you about David?"
"Of course" said my mom. "What is it?"

As I watched Mrs. Morris explain what happened today, I knew I was going to be doomed. I was going to get the lecture of my life with the punishment to match.

After my mom finished talking to Mrs. Morris, my mother sternly said, "Son, get in the car."

The entire way home no one made a sound. The radio wasn't even playing. We pulled up to the day care to get Aaden and my mother motioned for me to wait in the car while she went inside. When she returned to the car, she started to drive home but she still didn't make a sound. When we pulled into the driveway my mother's only words to me were, "David I'm very disappointed in you."
So that's it, I thought to myself. I'm disappointed in you David. No lecture. No punishment. Yes. King David scores! Video games here I come. Oh, and TV and board games.

"Whoo hoo" I yelled running towards the porch. Mrs. Morris must have not told my mom everything. Oh well, who cares! I'm free!
"Not so fast. I heard my dad say," but he couldn't have been talking to me so I kept running towards the porch.
"I said, not so fast young man! Your mom told me about your day at school. She and I are both very disappointed in you. I need you to understand when you behave in that manner you not only embarrass yourself but you embarrass every single member of this family. All of this because of Clucking Chicken?"
"Friggin Chicken."
"What?"
"The name of the game Dad. The name of the game is Friggin Chicken not Clucking Chicken."

"Oh so, Mr. Smart Guy, Mr. Funny Man corrects dad," he said **sarcastically**. Well, since you're so good at corrections you will have no trouble writing me a one page paper on the correct way to behave in school… and that's just the beginning of your punishment. First, you will write the paper. Next, you will get your room **immaculate**, including your closet and under your bed. Finally, you will clean out the entire garage. No games, no TV, no fun. Period!"
"But dad you didn't even ask me what happened."
"Absolutely positively no buts; straight to your room!"
"You and mom never listen to me. You always take someone else's side. I'm going to build me a rocket ship and go live on Mars and I'm not even going to visit on Thanksgiving and Christmas!"
I **bellowed**.

"Ah ha! This must be an example of the outburst you had today at school! You haven't learned your lesson yet? Oh, and by the way, there are rules everywhere you go, even on Mars. Now get to work!"

---

sarcastically (sar-cas-ti-cal-ly). adv. – expressing or marked by sarcasm; the use of irony to mock or convey contempt
immaculate (im-mac-u-late). adj.- perfectly clean, neat, or tidy
bellowed (bel-lowed). v. – emit a deep loud roar, typically in pain or anger

Friggin Chicken
Page 33

Again, David's Having Distractions

Chapter 8
I Hate Punishment

I spent the entire night writing a stupid paper instead of doing what I wanted to do. I never have any time to myself. Now, my father wakes me up at the butt crack of dawn to clean out the hot, stinky, smelly garage.

Boxes filled with clothes, tools, towels, and other useless junk. Dust, ants, granddaddy long legs... lawn mower junk, oil, car parts. I don't even know where to begin! It's going to take me until I'm 90 to finish cleaning up this place! And while I'm cleaning daddy and the rest of the "Perfects" are maxing and relaxing. Aren't there child labor laws for this kind of treatment? Ugh!, I screamed.

"Why are you yelling?" asked mom.
"...Because this is so unfair. I have to clean my life away while you guys have fun and it wasn't even my fault."
"Ah hem," mom cleared her throat.
"Okay, it wasn't entirely my fault."
"David, this is your punishment because you acted very inappropriately at school. You were rude, disrespectful, and disruptive."
"But you didn't even ask me what happened."
"Alright David. What happened?"

I began to tell my mom what happened even down to my disappearing act. When I was done she said, "David, I understand how you feel. However, that's no excuse and its sounds like it's all over a game. I agree with what your teacher said; Friggin Chicken is your game. You can make it as amazing or as boring as you want. Look around you David, there are all kinds of amazing things in this garage. Use your imagination."

What did she mean there are amazing things in this garage? It's nothing here but junk. I guess I will just clean up this mess.

Chapter 9
Mano y Mano

7:00 p.m. Finally done. I wonder what's next on Dad's horrible list of things for me to do.

"Hi David. You're just in time for dinner. Your mother just went to get pizza and soda with your brother and sister. This gives me a chance to talk to you mano y mano. Your mother told me your side of the events that happened at school and although I don't **condone** or agree with how you behaved, I do understand your reaction. I want you to tell me what happened in your own words."

I told my dad everything that happened; exactly how I told my mom. My dad's reaction was a little different from my mom's. My dad thought under no circumstances was my behavior understandable.

He also agreed with my mom. He said, "Your mom told me the advice she and your teacher gave you on your Fall Festival game. I think it was some great advice."
"Which part?"
"The part about you making it your own, and using your imagination to make it the best game there. I want you to come with me back to the garage. I want to show you something."
"Dad, I've been in the garage all day. I've seen everything there is to see. Please don't make me go back out there."
"Awe, come on son. It will be fun."

What could possibly be fun about digging around in a garage full of dusty boxes? I thought to myself; but this time I'm surely not

---

condone (con-done). v.- accept and allow to continue

going to open my mouth. It always seems to get me in trouble. So I followed my dad back to the garage and watched him search, dig through, and unorganize all the boxes I just finished straightening up.

"Ah ha! Here it is!" my dad shouted. "Here it is, son."
"Here's what, Dad?"
"Here is a picture of me holding a trophy from my first Cub Scout Pine Derby Race. I was ten years old and all the Cub Scouts had to make race cars out of wooden blocks. Once we shaped and sawed the cars we could paint and design them anyway we wanted. Well you know your dear old dad, right? This was a hard job for me. I'm not much of a car designer or decorator. Everyone else had turned their blocks of wood into really neat and cool cars. The kind of cars that you see on TV with really creative colors and decorations, and all I had was a block of wood but I was determined to be a part of the Pine Derby Race no matter what. So I took my wood home and I went into my father's shed and got some sandpaper and sawed my block of wood into a car. It was not as cool as the other boys but it was a car. Next, I found some paint and toy headlights and put them on my car. It didn't look like a television car but it was mine. I did my best and I was proud of it."

"When we raced our cars, I won 1st place in the derby and this trophy for having the most original car. Chi-ching."
"So what's the moral of the story David?"
"To make a block of wood into a car?," I asked sarcastically.
"Ha Ha. Wise guy. No, the moral of the story is to do your best, be creative, and make anything you work on your own. It's tons of stuff in here that can help you make Kickin' Chicken."
"Friggin Chicken Dad! Friggin Chicken!"
"Oh, excuse me Sir David. Friggin Chicken is an awesome game. Now put all this stuff back and think about what I said."
Honk. Honk. Beeeep.

"Your mother is back with dinner. Quickly put these things away and join us for dinner son."

"Pizza's here! Pizza's here! Pizza's here! I want two slices of extra cheese, chanted Miss Priss. And valilla ice cream."

"It's vanilla, you moron. Not valilla."

"You're the moron who has to spend the entire weekend cleaning up old junk crap."

"Hey! It's not crap! It's boxes filled with memories and wonderful stories," said dad. "Take this picture for example; I was just telling your brother the story behind this picture."

Emma quickly snatched the picture and examined the front and the back. "There's no story behind the picture daddy."

"No, not really behind the picture dear. The story that goes along with the picture."

"Moron," I whispered again. But she's the smart sixth grader- yeah right.

"See, I was 10 years old and a pretty cool kid if I must say so myself."

Then suddenly a loud crash cut my father off mid-sentence. Aaden had managed to turn over all the boxes on the bottom self. Spilling out everything that I had already put away and some stuff that was already nice and neat on the shelf.

"Oh my gosh!! Aaden you're just as clumsy and goofy as your brother, Brillo head, over here," said Emma.

"Aww Aaden, it's okay," mom said as she picked him up and kissed his fat, drooled covered cheeks. "It's okay baby. You're not goofy and clumsy. You're just a little busy body, that's all. And you watch your mouth young lady before you are cleaning up this garage with your brother."

"Wait! You mean to tell me that I have to not only clean up the mess dad came and created, but I have to clean up the mess Aaden made too? This has got to be some sort of joke! Come on, where are the hidden cameras?"

"I hate to be the **bearer** of bad news, but yes you do have clean up all this stuff... again," mom said with a serious facial expression like I've never seen. Now, come on gang. Let's eat. The pizza is getting cold. David, you can join us once this garage is cleaned properly... and before you open your mouth with one of your infamous quotes that always lands you in more trouble, just hush and get it clean."

"I guess you told me mom," I said because I just have to have the last word. "And while I'm at it why don't I change the oil, paint the house, mow the lawn, and clean the gutters."

"That sounds perfect David! Since you don't know how to keep your mouth closed you can do some of the wonderful things you just mentioned the rest of this week but for now just focus on the garage. O-kay."

"What? You really expect me to do all that stuff?"
"I told you to be quiet before you got yourself in more trouble but you always have to have the last word. Hopefully one day you'll learn your lesson, but for now, chop chop. We will save you some pizza."

---

bearer (bear-er). n. – a person or thing that carries or holds something

Chapter 10
It's Not All Junk

As I stood in disbelief at what my mom just said, I started plotting my ultimate revenge against this dreadful family.

First, I will pull all the heads off of Emma's dolls and bury them in the back yard. Next, I will fill my mother's shampoo bottle with green hair dye; that will make her look like the Incredible Hulk's little sister. Then, little droolie boy is next. I know exactly what to do to him. I will put egg juice in all of his baby bottles. He'll have gas for a whole year. I laughed aloud to myself. And finally I will save the best for last; my dear old dad!! I will destroy all his old junk memories in these boxes. I will take 'em to the beach and watch them sink to the bottom of the ocean. Starting with this box right here, I said while taking a swift kick to one of the old boxes. "Ouch! That hurt!"

This box feels like a ton of bricks. How did Aaden manage to pull this down? What's in here?, I thought to myself.
More of my dad's junk probably. Hey, guess what David you're not only smart but you're psychic because it is just more of my dad's junk in this box. Large rubber bands, feathers, small wheels, papers, buttons- --what was he doing with all this stuff I wonder? Building a paper chicken?!?

Wait! Wait a minute! A chicken? If I take this, this, and add that; then... Oh boy!!
I quickly cleaned the garage in record time; everything except for what I found in that box. I ran inside with the box and dashed upstairs.

"David, we saved some pizza for you," yelled mom.

"No time to eat mom! There are more important things to do!"
"That kid sure is strange," said Emma with a mouthful of pizza.
"Well, whatever he's doing it must be pretty important to pass up pizza," dad said as he crammed one of the slices they saved for me in his mouth.

Chapter 11
Banana Pancakes

Finally, I'm done! I can't believe I stayed up so late working on this. Grrrrr. My stomach can't believe it either.
I wonder if there's any pizza left. I'll go downstairs to check.
Nope. No pizza left, but I think it's some left over mac 'n cheese in the fridge.

Umm... I don't see it. It's not behind the milk or behind the left over tuna noodle casserole. "Where is it?" I belted out!
"What's going on down there? David is that you? What's all that noise?"
"Yes, mom. It's me. I got so caught up with working that I forgot to eat."
"Do you have any idea what time it is son?"
"I know, but no one saved me any pizza. So I wanted to eat the left over mac n cheese but that's gone too" I said as I placed my head on the kitchen table.
"Aww David, I'm sorry. We did eat all the pizza because you ran to your room in such haste, and I threw all the macaroni and cheese out this morning. Would you like me to make you some of my famous banana pancakes, kiddo? Just me and you – a little late night snack?"
"Really mom? You're not gonna say it's too late?"
"No David, it's not too late. It's the perfect time for my favorite middle child and pancakes. Hey, maybe you can even tell me what you were in your room working on."
"Can I have a glass of milk too, please?"
"Of course David. Here you are dear."
"Thanks," I said after taking a big gulp.
"Um. So you were up there working all this time- on the game for

Fall Festival I **presume**?"

"That's top secret, but what I can tell you is I found some really cool stuff that Dad had in the garage."

"Ahh in the garage, aye... umm hmm. I see- exactly the place I suggested you look initially, huh? So what kind of stuff did you find? What did you use it for? Does your dad know what you were up to? Don't keep me on edge David! Tell me about what you were so **diligently** working on," she asked as she sat down at the table with me.

"Okay. Okay. Okay mom *geesh*. You're asking so many questions! I will tell you, but first pancakes *pleassszzzah*."
"Sure thing, King David," she said with a slight giggle.
"So mom, you know how you guys forced me to clean the garage; which by the way I'm almost positive there are child labor laws that protect against that sorta thing."
"Alright David, don't **digress** just stick to the facts."
"Well, like I was saying I was cleaning the garage and I noticed this one particular box that was sort of heavy. I looked in the box and saw all kinds of neat things that I could use to make Friggin Chicken the best game ever. Not only the best game ever but the best game in the entire school. Good enough to win first prize at Fall Festival."

"David, I would love to know what all the hoopla has been about. Is it that top secret that you can't tell me a little bit about it?"
"Ugh. Okay mom gosh! Friggin Chicken is a game that is similar to horseshoes. The contestant has to be blindfolded, spins around in a circle, and then tosses the chicken. Whoever tosses the chicken the furthest wins."

---

presume (pre-sume). v. – to take for granted as being true in the absence of proof to the contrary
diligently (dil-i-gent-ly). adj. – having or showing care and conscientiousness in one's work or duties
digress (di-gress). v. – leave the main subject temporarily in speech or writing

Again, David's Having Distractions

"Sounds interesting but how do you win if you are the host of the game."

"I win if my game collects the most tickets; if my game line stretches for miles and miles and miles- that will show everyone that my game is a hit. Michael Hunter will lose. TO ME!! I will finally be able to say I beat him at something," I said with my most fierce game face stare.

"Oh my! This sounds very interesting, but don't tell me all of this drama has been about beating some kid?"

"Yeah? Sort of," I said while I swallowed a mouthful of my mom's fluffy banana pancakes.

"Yeah?"

"Oh, I mean yes ma'am."

"David you have been put out of class, yelled at, and punished all because of some rival between you and this Hunter kid?"

"Yeah. Sort of."

"Yeah again?"

"No. I mean yes ma'am."

"Well I think it's safe to assume that you have learned a couple of valuable lessons from all of this, right?"

"Uh huh, yes mom. Some very, very valuable lessons," I said while blinking my eyes hoping that she wouldn't ask me what those lessons are.

"Uh hm and those lessons are"...

"First, ramble through the garage whenever Fall Festival comes for old junk for crappy games."

"Second, announce my greatness no matter what comes my way."

"Third, uh tell Michael Hunter I'm number one," I said while shrugging my shoulders.

"That's one way to look at it David, but let's try the humble approach. I think it is important for you to understand that number one: no matter the game or task you receive you should always do your best and be creative. You are an Allen and we always do our best. Secondly, instead of announcing your greatness what about being quiet and not disrupting class and AND discussing your concerns with your teacher after class is over. Respectfully. Third, you should end this silly rival with Michael Hunter because you seem to be the one that gets into all of the trouble and finally, know when to debate an issue and when to be quiet."

"That's some good advice your mom just gave you," said dad as he walked into the kitchen.
"What are you guys doing up? *And* eating mom's famous banana pancakes?"

"I heard David down here rambling in the refrigerator after working so rigorously in his room. He was hungry so I made him a little snack."
"Wait a minute here. You were in your room *working*?"
"Yes, I said swallowing a gulp of milk."
"Working on what?"

"It's top secret," I said smiling at mom.
"Yes, it's top secret she winked back. Let's go back to bed honey."
"Good night mom. Good night dad."
"Good night son. Oh and put your dishes away and go straight to bed- it's after midnight."

Chapter 12
Hard Work Doesn't Always Pay Off

Mmm. Those pancakes really hit the spot but who can sleep at a time like this. Now I'm recharged and ready to do some more work.

"First I'm going to lay here for a few minutes and collect all my thoughts," I said with a deep yawn. Or maybe I will take a quick nap then get right up. I will set my alarm for one hour from now. Then it will be back to work.
Knock. Knock. Knock.

"Wake up cheese head. Your alarm clock has been ringing all night. Mom and Dad said get up and shut it off."
"Did ya hear me? Mom and Dad said GET UP!!"
"*Heyyy*, what are you doing in here? What's with all the feathers and wheels."

"Emma, if you don't get out of my room I'm going to pound you into mashed potatoes."
"Pound me? I think not! I'm the oldest; which means I'm bigger than you, stronger than you, and I'm definitely smarter than you."
Thwaaap
"*Waaaaaaah.* Mom, Dad! David pushed me on the floor and all I was doing was trying to wake him like you told me to."
"You guys don't start up this morning! Emma stop being an **antagonist** to your brother and David don't hit your sister. I want you two to come downstairs I have a surprise for the family."
"Yes mom."

---

antagonist (an-tag-o-nist). n. – a person who actively opposes or is hostile to someone or something

Again, David's Having Distractions

"Move out my way Brillo head and brush your teeth. Your morning breath is toxic."

"What's your excuse? You've been up all morning!"

"Stop it you two! I have an announcement to make. Now, since everyone is here, I had an idea that will allow all of us to have some fun today."

"Fun? Today? I thought I was on punishment."

"Yeah. I thought guacamole breath was on punishment."

"He is on punishment and this is part of it. Our family is going to have a mini Fall Festival!"

"A what?"

"A mini Fall Festival. David is going to test his game out on us."

"MOM, I TOLD YOU THAT WAS TOP SECRET!"

"I know David but I want to be sure that when you host the game at school there are no major glitches. Besides whenever anyone creates a new product they should always test it out- especially to people they know. You know, for feedback. All major corporations do it. This is no different."

"Mom this is home, not work. Who cares about feedback and corporations? This is a top secret mission."

"Aww, come on David! It will be fun. I have two more games set up outside just to make things more fun. Come on everyone, let's go take a look".

"Over here we have darts and on this side we have balloon pop. Doesn't that sound like fun?"

"*Nooo*!" Emma and I said together. For once we agreed on something.

"Good thing I have the final say. Go brush your teeth and let's get started."

"Ugh mom and her great ideas. Then I told her it was top secret. What is she thinking? Why is she doing this? Michael Hunter better not show up and who's going to host those other games? Drooling boy and Miss Pigtails? And isn't this country a democracy? Aren't we supposed to vote for the final say so? Puhh!"

"Sorry son, democracy ended when you walked through the front door," said dad as he grabbed the toothpaste. "This house is called the United States of the Awesome Allens. I'm the king and your mom is the queen."

"Oh and so what the rest of us are just peasants; mere villagers under the rule of the **domineering** king and queen?"

"Domineering- that's a good word son. Glad to see that you're learning something in school. Way to stretch that vocabulary. Now wipe your mouth and let's go."

Did my parents just totally overlook the fact that I wanted to keep this game under wraps until game day-that I didn't want to reveal what I have done to guarantee my shot at being number one. This is so unfair, but if it's a game they want then a game they'll get.

---

domineering (dom-i-neer-ing). v. – assert one's will over another in an arrogant way

Chapter 13
Family Works

"So nice of you to finally join us David. Did you bring your chicken game down? I have an area for you to set up right over there. While David's setting up, I'm going to explain how this works. Each person will have a chance to play each game, including the host. After everyone has had a turn, then we will all vote for which game is the best. We will have a secret ballot to decide who wins. If, at the end of voting, there is a tie, the winner will be based on the amount of fun the participants were having according to my personal observations. Dad, you're hosting darts and Emma, you're hosting balloon pop."

"Mom, this doesn't make any sense. If dad, David and I are hosting the game, then the only players are you and Aaden. How is that 'family fun'?"

"You guys just follow my lead-watch and see- we are going to have loads of fun."

"First up is darts! Everybody get in line except for Dad and my slobby baby. You're too small for these games. Sit here in your bouncer and make sure your brother and sister don't try to make a quick escape."

"Why doesn't dad have to get in line and play this dumb game?"
"Excuse, me but this game is not dumb. It's fun and everybody is going to enjoy it. Is that understood?"
"Yes ma'am."
"And if you and your sister had been listening I said everyone including the host will take a turn. Now everyone get over here and hustle. Emma you're first."
"Gee whiz mom is so bossy," Emma whispered. This was the one time my sister and I were allies.

"Alright little lady grab a dart and aim for the bull's eye. Everyone will have one turn to hit the bull's eye. Ready...set....GO!"

Emma quickly threw the dart at the dart board but she missed.

"Sorry Emma, you were too low. The dart didn't even come close to the dart board. Next up is David."

"Oh mom! Do I have to?"

"Yes, you surely do! Now grab a dart."

"Ready. Aim. Throw."

"Alright, 40 points!! Good David. So right now the score is 40 points to everyone's zero."

"Next up is mom."

I wondered why she was announcing herself. She is way too into this game.

"Alright, got my dart. Ready. Aim. Throw."

"Alright 30 points! David still has the lead. Last person with a possible chance at a win is Dad. Come on Dad grab a dart."

"Yeah dad, get a dart and beat big head David."

"Okay. okay. okay. I'll take this dart *riiiiight* here- looks like a winner," dad said with a slight smirk.

"Okay dear. Ready. Aim. Throw."

"Bull's eye! We have our winner of the first game."

"Oh wow dad, you hit the Bull's eye," said Emma.

"Way to go, honey."

"Da da da da," said Aaden trying to **mimic** everyone else.

"David, aren't you going to congratulate your father?"

Congratulate him?, I thought to myself. No I don't want to congratulate dad. It was clear he was going to win. He's bigger than me, faster and stronger than me. This is cheating at its finest.

"Hello, David. Did you hear me? Congratulate your father on winning darts."

"David is sour about losing again, and now that you have proven that and Dad has won, can we go inside so I can watch television."

"Surely your sister can't be right? I thought we had a long talk about losing and the proper attitude to have."

---

mimic (mim-ic). v. – imitate

"I know mom but don't you think dad winning is a tad bit unfair?"
"No, I do not. Now congratulate your father or you will be
cleaning the attic next for poor sportsmanship."
"Okay. Alright. Congratulations." I mumbled.
"Excuse me, we couldn't hear you."
"I SAID, congratulations dad on winning the game!"
I had to admit hitting the bull's eye on the first try was pretty cool,
I thought to myself. My dad has skills.
"Next up is Balloon Pop. Emma you're the host of this game."
"I've set up four chairs across the lawn. Each one has a balloon in
the seat. The object of the game is to be the first person to pop their
balloon by sitting on it."
"What about Aaden?"

"I have a small rubber ball in the grass that he can play with so he
doesn't feel left out. I will set the timer for 15 seconds. As soon as
we hear the ring, we can begin trying to pop the balloons."
"Sounds easy to me," I said.

"Okay everyone stand in front of a chair and you mister, Aaden boo, sit here with your ball and make sure no one cheats- muuu-waah," mom said kissing him on the cheek.

"Timer set, everybody listen for the ring."
We have 15 seconds, I thought to myself. If I start counting down now, by the time the timer reaches 14 seconds I can start squatting closer to my balloon and become the ultimate winner!
Ringgggggg

Dang those 15 seconds went by fast. I didn't even have time to count. Everyone began bouncing up and down trying to pop the balloons but no one has been able to pop it.
"Come on David, sit harder," mom said while laughing.
"Yeah David, sit down harder," Dad said as he bounced his self right onto the ground.
Emma was laughing so hard she couldn't even bounce at all. And me? Well, the harder I bounced the harder the balloon bounced back. But I had to admit this game sure is fun.
Then suddenly, *POP*!!!!
Mom managed to pop her balloon.
"I won! I won!" Mom sang.
"Everyone congratulate your mother on her win even you mister baby boy. Give mommy a congratulations kiss."
"Muah, thank you Aaden."
"Congratulations mom," said Emma while still trying pop her balloon.
"Yeah, congrats mom," I said while giving her a hug.
"Now it's time for David's game. I don't know the rules to this game so can you explain them to all of us."
"First, you have to pick the chicken you want to throw. After everyone has their own chicken you have to spin around in a circle ten times and then throw the chicken. Which ever chicken goes the furthest wins. That's it!"
"Seems pretty simple to me."

"Alright everybody grab a chicken. On the count of three every-body start spinning."
1… 2…. 3…..

Everyone start spinning as fast as they could to reach 10 spins. I was first. Fling. My chicken went flying in the air. Next went my Mom's, then Dad's, and finally Emma's.
"Ugh, the wheels came off of mine," shouted Emma.
"The feathers got caught between my wheels," said dad.
And all the feathers came off and all the wheels came of off mine and mom's. None of the chickens even went far. What gives?! I stayed up all night working on this game.
"This game sucks and you're gonna lose at Fall Festival. You better play sick or runaway," said Emma laughing.
"Shut up, before I make you eat dirt Emma."
But Emma was right. This game did suck and I am going to lose in front of the entire school, including Michael Hunter.

"Mom, can we go in now? We all know who the winner is. Dad's game was okay, David's game sucked, and my game rocked."
"What did I tell you about your mouth young lady? Drop and give me twenty."

"Why am I being punished? I told the truth. His game fell apart right before our own eyes."
"Make that twenty-five and if you don't hush you will lose all your television privileges for the week."
As Emma began doing her push-ups, I began picking up the pieces to my game. I don't get it. This game was supposed to be a hit. The feathers were supposed to make the chickens fly further and the wheels were supposed to make it glide once it hit the ground. But everything just fell apart.
"Here David," said Dad handing me the wheels and feathers from one of the chickens. "Are you alright? Don't let your sister get to you."

"I'm fine Dad, but Emma is kinda right. I put a lot of hard work into this game and it just didn't work out. Guess the only thing left for me to do is be **humiliated** in front of the entire school. I hope all of you are happy. Dr. Jackson and Mrs. Morris will get a big kick out of this."

"David, have you ever heard of Tommy Smith?"

"Who?"

"Okay- what about John Carlos?"

"Uhh, can't say that I have."

"Well, I know you've heard of Michael Jordan, right?"

"You mean Michael Jackson Dad. What does pop music have to do with a chicken game?"

"Not Michael Jackson- Michael Jordan the greatest basketball player ever."

"Oh yeah, you mean the guy with all the tennis shoes you never buy me. What does he have to do with flying chickens? I should have used tennis shoes instead of wheels?"

"No. Michael Jordan, John Carlos, and Tommy Smith are all famous athletes who had to overcome lots of challenges to become successful. Michael Jordan even got cut from a team before he made it. He kept practicing and trying until he got better. He didn't stop at the first sign of defeat."

"This story would be great if I was trying to be a famous chicken thrower or a professional chicken guy. Friggin Chicken is a dumb game and I'm going to the laughing stock of the entire school. I took you guys advice and tried to make this game my own and it fell apart."

"Alright then David, have it your way," Dad said handing me the last few pieces that was left on the ground. If you want to give up and be a quitter the first time things don't go right then be my guess but don't expect any **empathy** from me."

---

humiliated (hu-mil-i-ate-d). v. – make feel ashamed and foolish by injuring their dignity

em·pa·thy [em-puh-thee] n. the attribution to an object, such as a work of art, of one's own emotional or intellectual feelingsabout it

Again, David's Having Distractions

As I watched Dad walk away, I wondered three things: Why he doesn't understand me? What in the world is empathy, and why didn't he have any for me?

As the day went on, I stayed in my room only coming out for lunch and dinner. While in my room, I stared at all the chickens in the box and imagined my downfall at school tomorrow. The older kids and the younger kids will have a time making fun of me, King Chicken Sandwich. Michael Hunter, Ashley, and the rest of my class will have a field day all at my expense. Maybe I can make my way back to the supply closet. I rather get into trouble from being in the supply closet than to be embarrassed in front of the entire school.

Knock. Knock. Knock.
Someone is knocking at my door and I'm too annoyed to talk to anyone- especially my mom and Dad.
Knock. Knock. Knock.
 "David it's me, Emma. Can I come in?"
"No!" I shouted. "I don't want to talk to you or anyone else in this family."

"Well, that's too bad David because I'm coming in anyway!"
"I SAID I DON'T WANNA TALK!"
"And I SAID tough. I was just coming up to see if you wanted ice cream before you went to bed."
"No thanks."

"You've been in here **sulking** all day. I don't see what the big deal is anyway. It's just a game; a game with flying chickens- that in itself is funny and makes the game a hit."
"Thanks Emma for trying to cheer me up, but you don't get it either. You don't understand what it's like to be me. You have the perfect hair, perfect grades, perfect friends, and you're the perfect

---

sulking (sulk-ing). v. –be silent, morose, and bad tempered out of annoyance or disappointment

child. Perfect!"

"David I would love to join you and your pity party if I believed any of those things to be true, but since they are not, I won't. Your hair is fine, your grades are fine, and so is everything else."
"If my hair is fine, why do you insist on calling me Brillo head every chance you get?"

"That's what I'm supposed to do. I'm big sis. I'm supposed to give you a hard time, cheese breath," Emma said while laughing. "You have two hours until bedtime why don't you try gluing all the parts back on the chickens and whatever else happens tomorrow happens. It's not the end of the world."

As my sister left my room, I thought about what she said. Whatever happens- it's not the end of the world. If Carlos Jordan or whoever my dad was talking about can do it, then so can I.

Chapter 14
Doom's Day

"Wake up honey. You forgot to set your alarm. We're running a tad bit late. Get dressed fast. We'll have breakfast in the car. Don't forget your book bag and stuff for your game, and oh, grab an umbrella. It looks like rain today."

What?! Rain? This is a dream come true. Rain means no Fall Festival. I hurried and got dressed brushed my teeth, and had a bowl of cereal for breakfast. I grabbed my book bag, box of chickens, and my umbrella. I ran outside only to see that everything was bone dry.

"What gives?" I asked aloud. I went back inside and yelled upstairs to my mom, "I thought you said it was raining."

"No honey, I said it looks like rain" she yelled back down the stairs.

"*Are you dressed already?*" She said kind of surprised walking down the stairs.

"Yes."

"That sure was fast. Fastest ever," she said smiling and rubbing my hair.

"Mom stop messing up my hair and why would you say anything about rain?"

"I don't know David. I thought it would be smart to have an umbrella just in case it starts to rain. What's the big deal anyway?"

"Because if it rained that meant..." I took a long pause.

"Meant what?"

"Never mind."

I wasn't in the mood for a lecture or a pep talk. So I didn't want to tell her why I was so excited about rain. I guess I will have to just take Emma's advice and let whatever happens, happen.

"Come on guys your brother is ready, let's go".

"I'm sitting in the front," shouted Emma.

I didn't put up a fight at all. The only thing I could focus on was Fall Festival and this chicken game. Mom dropped Aaden off first, the Emma at her Charter School for smart, fancy kids. Last to get dropped off was me. Before getting out of the car mom had this look on her face like she was going to give me a speech or something. So I sat there and prepared myself for the whole **ordeal**.
"David."
"Yes mom."
"I'm sorry that your game fell apart. Very sorry."
"Really mom? Does this mean I don't have to go to school?"
"As I was saying, I'm very sorry that your game fell apart, and I think that it would be a good idea if the family came to Fall Festival to support you. Maybe me, dad, sis, and Aaden could help host and be there if anybody makes fun of you."
"Sure mom. That would be great. Not only will the entire school be laughing at me but they will be laughing at my entire family too-we will be the chicken sandwich family!"
"No need to get sassy- it was just a suggestion David."
"Great suggestion," I said sarcastically. "See you at noon."
As I got out of the car and closed the door, I looked at the sky to see if maybe it was a gray cloud or even a slight **trickle** of rain, but nope- nothing- bone dry. I saw Mrs. Morris going into the school at the same time as me.
"Good morning, David."
"Good morning."

"I see you have your game and it looks like you have added some extra flare to the game too! I can't wait to see all the great games today. How about you?"
"Yeah, I can hardly wait," I said sarcastically.
We walked down the hallway together and some of my classmates were already waiting by the door.

---

ordeal (or-deal). n. – a painful or horrific experience
trickle (trick-le). n. - a small flow of liquid

"Hey, look there's chicken boy!" said one kid. "And look, he laid eggs and has a bunch of chicken babies."

Several students outside the class started laughing. I didn't even turn to see who made the joke.

"Alright, you will not be participating in Fall Festival for that negative comment young man and anyone else who thinks it's funny to tease other kids."

"Teasing is what, class?"

"A FORM OF BULLYING!"

"And this school has what tolerance for bullying?"

"ZERO!"

She took out her key, unlocked the door and let everyone in the class except for me. She stopped me at the door and reminded me to keep my cool and not to let others bother me. Also, she informed me that if anyone made fun of me she would not let them participate in the games.

I don't really see how this helped me. I still had to participate and risk being humiliated in front of the entire school.

It was 7:45 and the morning bell rang. Everyone was in class including Michael Hunter. Everyone had their game supplies by their desks. Mrs. Morris told the class that we will be having a free day since it was Fall Festival. She said we would watch two movies before the games began. But, to make sure we were still learning she wanted us to write the plot, setting, and main characters in each movie.

"Class, the first movie we are going to watch is Madagascar. Then we're going to watch Shrek. Can someone tell me the overall setting of Madagascar?"

All hands flew up except mine.

"Okay Ashley."

"Africa."

"Yes, you are correct."

"Now, can someone tell me what the theme to the movie Shrek is?"

No one raised their hand.

"Alright, well I guess I will have to just call on someone. Let me see here."

I slumped down so far in my seat that I was eye level with my desk.

"Michael Hunter what is the theme to the movie Shrek?"

"I don't know Mrs. Morris. I have never seen the movie Shrek."

"Okay. Let me call on someone else. David."

Ugh I knew it, I thought to myself.

"Yes."

"What is the theme to the movie Shrek?"

"Uhhh. Can you repeat the question?"

"WHAT IS THE THEME TO THE MOVIE SHREK?"

"*Welllll, ummm*, the theme to the movie Shrek is *uhhhmmm-* never grow up to be an ogre? Yeah that's it. Never grow up to be an ogre."

"More like never grow up to be a chicken sandwich!"

The entire class laughed.

"Who said that? I want to know who said that."

The entire class remained silent.

"Another outburst like that and no one will participate in Fall Festival."

I had my fingers crossed for another outburst. Maybe if I stand up and do the funky chicken everyone in the class will start picking on me. Wait, that's a good idea. I will flap my arms and squawk like a chicken. Surely that will get me kicked out of Fall Festival.

Bwak, bwa, bwa, bwa, bwa, bwa. Cluck, cluck, cluck, cluck.

Everyone in the class stared at me, but no one made a peep. So I squawked louder.

Bwak, BWAK, BWAK, BWAK.

"Mr. Allen, can I see you outside please?"

"Yes, bwak you can Mrs. Morris," I answered back still squawking and flapping around like a chicken.

As she closed the door behind her, we heard the entire class roar with laughter.

"I know exactly what you are trying to do mister, but there is absolutely nothing you can do to make me remove you from the games. So, you can continue to make a mockery of yourself- you only make yourself look silly."

"But you said any more outbursts and no one will be participating."

"No one except for you! Now can you please stop chicken walking so we all can enjoy the movie?"

As Mrs. Morris and I walked back inside, the class was silent except for a few low giggles in the back of the class.
"Now that everyone is acting normally, let's begin the movie."

Again, David's Having Distractions

Chapter 15
Saved by the Rain

At the end of Madagascar everyone took out a sheet of paper and wrote down the characters, theme, plot, and setting like Mrs. Morris told us to. As everyone turned in their paper, I couldn't help but to think about what was going to happen after the next movie- the end of King David.

"David, stop daydreaming and turn in your seatwork so we can begin the next show," said Mrs. Morris.

I got up and began walking towards her desk when I heard the most amazing sound- thunder! It was about to start raining. This was perfect timing! I handed Mrs. Morris my seatwork and couldn't help but smile, but she returned my smile with a disappointed frown. As I walked back to my seat, I heard the amazing sound again!

BOOM!

The glorious sound of thunder and whenever there's thunder there is surely lightening. That combination guarantees that there will be no Fall Festival.

"I'm about to start Shrek. Everyone take out another sheet of paper to write down the same things you wrote previously for Madagascar."

Beep Due to the inclement weather we will not be having our annual Fall Festival. Again, due to the inclement weather we *will not be having our annual Fall Festival. *Beep**

Oh no! Aww man! Shouted several students in the class.
All I could think was Oh yes! I didn't have to host this chicken game.

"Alright settle down class- the movie is starting."

The entire time the movie was playing I thought about how I had just escaped being the school's laughing stock. I was so happy I actually wanted to jump up and do a real chicken dance. I guess Mrs. Morris could tell what I was thinking because she was giving me the same look my mom gives me when she's frustrated with me. But it was nothing she could do so, I continued to smile and watch the movie.

Shrek was almost over and I couldn't help but wonder what we're going to do for the rest of the day. Since Fall Festival was cancelled she had no choice but to give us a free day.

Oh boy! I thought to myself. This surely was turning out to be a great day.

Chapter 16
Mrs. Morris' Great Idea

The movie was almost over and the rain sure was pouring down outside. Most of my classmates were whispering to each other and passing notes about how they were upset they were that Fall Festival had been cancelled. Normally, Mrs. Morris doesn't allow the class to whisper and pass notes while a movie is playing but this time she wasn't saying anything.

I glanced over at her desk and noticed she was writing something on a piece of paper. Then she called Michael to her desk, handed him the paper, and then he left the classroom.
I wonder what's that was about. Maybe she caught him passing notes and gave him an office referral. No, she probably had him go to the library to get more movies for our free day.
Yeah, that's it! More movies! This is going to be the best day ever!
Michael returned to the classroom and gave Mrs. Morris a thumbs up, but he didn't have any movies.

Then all of a sudden *Beep* *Hello teachers, students, faculty, and staff; one of our wonderful teachers suggested that we have our Fall Festival in the gym. I thought this was an excellent idea. However, since the gym has limited space, each class can only choose four games to represent their class. Let the games* **commence** *in thirty minutes* *Beep*.

The entire class cheered at the announcement given by the principal and Mrs. Morris had a big smile on her face.

---

commence (com-mence). v. – begin; start

"I wonder how she's going to pick," whispered Megan to Michael. "I wonder if we will have to play fastest draw," he whispered back. I wondered too. Since only four of us get to host a game, then maybe she will spare me and allow a student who really wants to represent our class.

"Students, we have only a few minutes to decide who will represent our class for Fall Festival. Two girls and two boys will be allowed to represent us. If you would like to participate please raise your hand."

Everyone raised their hand.
"Oh my, so many hands how will I ever choose."
My hand was the only hand that wasn't impatiently waving in the air. But, if I raised it, then she might think I'm over being embarrassed about the game and choose someone else.
"I'm so excited to see all these eager hands, but everyone please put your hands down. I am going to make my decision based on the games I think will help us win Fall Festival."
This is awesome because everyone knows Friggin Chicken is the worse game. It's no way in the world she would choose me even if she picked Michael Hunter.
"First up is Sit n Spin hosted by Cara. Next, is Long Ranger hosted by Ashley. Third to represent our class is Slam Dunk You hosted by Michael Hunter, and last but not least is Friggin Chicken hosted by David Allen."
"What? I thought you said you were going to choose games that you thought will help us win."
"I did David," she said with a big smile.
This was trickery at its best. I should have known Mrs. Morris was plotting something. She was too calm and too quiet when the other students were talking and passing notes during the movie. I guess it's fate. I'm supposed to be the laughing stock of the entire school.

Chapter 17
School Jester

"Everyone turn in your assignment and get in line. Ashley, Cara, David, and Michael get all the materials for your games and let's head to the gymnasium."

On the way to the gym I noticed other classes on their way to the gym, and just like our class four students in each class had a box with all their game stuff in it.

One fifth graders blurted out, "Hey look at chicken boy. Bet he's going sit on a chicken and lay an egg."

The hallway filled with laughter from the fifth graders and from everyone in my class. It was already beginning! I was the laughing stock.

Mrs. Morris quickly stepped in and got everyone to quiet down, but the damage had already been done. I, King David was going to be the jester.
When we arrived at the gym several classes were already setting up. Each class had their own section for their game, and the students who weren't hosting were seated on the bleachers.
"David and Michael you can set up over there and you girls can take this space right here."

As we were setting up, I noticed some students' parents and siblings began to show up including mine. Just great I thought to myself. My entire family is here. Just in time for them to see the king transformed into a jester. At this point it really didn't matter who was here and who wasn't here. I was doomed.

After everyone set up each game, Dr. Jackson told everyone to begin having fun, and to enjoy the snacks. There was a cotton candy stand, a hot dog stand, and other kinds of cool treats. The snack lines were longer than the game lines, which was great news for me.

"Step right up. Step right up. Come play Slam Dunk You," shouted Michael into the crowd. He wasn't the only one- all the game hosts were chanting different thing trying to get people to come play their game; everyone except for me.

"Step right up. Step right up." Michael continued shouting.
"Ah, finally my first customer. Hello, how are you sir?"
"I'm fine. How do you play this game?"
"I give you three balls and you try to hit the bull's eye. If you hit the bull's eye, you will slam dunk my assistant, Dana, into the water. If you slam dunk her in the water, then you will win a prize."
"Sounds simple to me!"
"Okay sir. Start throwing whenever you're ready."
"You're never going to hit the bull's eye you're too old, too slow, and too ugly" heckled Dana.
The gamer threw his first ball.
"Oh, he missed," chuckled Michael. "He missed. You have two more balls left."

"You might as well give those balls back to Michael, Grandpa. You're never gonna slam dunk me."
The contestant throws the second ball…
"Oh no! He misses the bull's eye again! I'm starting to think Dana's right. Maybe you are too old and too slow Grandpa. You have one last chance to slam dunk Dana into the ooey gooey, nasty water tank. Come on everyone, let's cheer him on."
Go, go, go, go, go, chanted everyone in the gym.
"No matter how many cheers you get you still will suck. You throw

like a girl and you look like *aaaaaaaaaa*"…

"Slam Dunk You!" shouted the contestant.

"He hit the bull's eye everybody! He hit the *bullzzz eyeeee*. You can choose from any of these prizes."

"Alright, step right up. Who's next? Who wants a chance to slam dunk Dana into the water tank?"

Michael's line was getting long, which made me happy and angry at the same time. I was happy because this meant no one would want to play this lame ole chicken game. I was mad because this meant I wouldn't win best game for Fall Festival… AGAIN! Maybe if I scream "*rat*," everyone would run and panic. Then, Dr. Jackson would have to cancel Fall Festival. Or maybe I could fall down and pretend I broke my leg, and they would say I won by default. Or maybe, just maybe…

"Excuse me David. I hate to interrupt your day dreaming, but I would like to play your game," said Mrs. Morris handing me a ticket.

"But I didn't say step right up," I replied hoping she would just go away before anyone else came along.

"That's true David, you did not say step right up but that's not required to play a game; so here's my ticket. Now, hand me a chicken!"

"Okay, but for this game we need at least two players and since no one else wants to play this game you can't either."

"I bet we could find someone else to play this game with me. Didn't I see your family here? I bet Emma would love to play with me and look she's right there sitting down doing nothing!"

"Emma darling, would you be a doll and play your brother's game with me? We need at least two players."

"Sure Mrs. Morris, but I must warn you this game really sucks. We tried it at home and everything fell apart. I thought it was funny,

but Mom made me do push-ups because I laughed."
"You have such a big mouth Emma," I said.
"Cry baby!" she shouted back.
"And an ugly face to match," I said.

"Here are your Friggin Chickens. Have fun!"
While Emma explained the rules to Mrs. Morris, I looked around
to see if anyone else was getting in line to play this stupid game.
Thankfully, there wasn't a person in sight, and hopefully it will
stay that way.

As Emma and Mrs. Morris began spinning in a circle, I heard
Michael Hunter yell, "Hey everybody, look! Somebody is actually
playing the clucking plucking game." All the students in the gym
began to laugh **hysterically**.

"The only two people in the entire gym who even wanted to play
that lame ole game is a teacher and his sister. They must have felt
sorry for the cheese head."

"Or maybe he paid them," heckled Dana, along with Michael
Hunter.

"Come on everyone. Let's watch this plucking chucking game."
"Why don't you mind your own beez wax dragon foot face?" I
shouted at Michael. "Host your game and I will host mine!"
By the time Michael and I finished exchanging words almost
everyone's attention was on me, Emma, Mrs. Morris and Friggin
Chicken. Emma and Mrs. Morris had already picked the chickens
they wanted and were waiting on me to start the game. At this
point, there wasn't anything I could do to save myself from the
embarrassment that was about to take place. No matter what I did
they were going to play this game and I was going to be the
laughing stock of the entire school.

---

hysterically (hys-ter-i-cal-ly). adj. – affected by uncontrolled extreme emotion

"Come on David! We're waiting on you," said Mrs. Morris.
"Alright, Alright, Alright. When I say go, start spinning in a circle as fast as you can and then release the chicken. Whoever's chicken goes the furthest wins."

"Okay!" Emma and Mrs. Morris said together.
"Ready. Set. Go!!"

They both spun around as fast as they could ten times. After they were done spinning, they both were staggering and wobbling trying to get their balance.

All of the students were laughing in amusement because Emma and Mrs. Morris were so dizzy.

Even though they were stumbling they both released their chickens into the air. Both of the chickens came down and crashed onto the floor at the same time. I thought for sure this would be the moment that I would become the joke of the entire school. I thought for sure the wheels and feathers would fall off just like they did when I tried it at home.

The entire gym was silent. Then suddenly someone yelled, "...that chicken is doing doughnut spins. Whoa!!"

"Look, the other chicken is drifting!"shouted another student.

The wheels were making the chickens glide and drift and the feathers were helping them to move faster. This was **aerodynamics** at its finest.

"Cool!" shouted another kid.

After the chickens stopped gliding and drifting they still had enough speed and force to continue moving forward.

"Emma's is going to win," shouted Dana.

"No, Mrs. Morris' chicken is moving way faster than Emma's," yelled Megan.

The chickens continued spinning and moving faster and faster. Emma's chicken **veered** to the left, but Mrs. Morris' chicken veered to the right. They both came to a complete stop at the same time, but it was hard to tell which one went the furthest.

"How can we tell whose went the furthest?" asked Emma. "They went in two different directions."

"Let's get a measuring tape," said Mrs. Morris.

She went to the supply closet and pulled out a measuring tape that could measure at least 100 feet. She laid the tape down and began measuring from the spot they began spinning. She went to Emma's chicken first.

"Emma your chicken went 33 feet! Whoa! That's impressive. Now, let's measure mine. David you get the measuring tape so you kids can't say I cheated," Mrs. Morris said jokingly.

I got the measuring tape and began measuring from the same spot Mrs. Morris began. I walked in the direction of her chicken and noticed that the numbers were getting higher and higher.

---

aerodynamics (aer-o-dy-nam-ics). n. – the study of the properties of moving air; the interaction between air and solid bodies moving through it

veered (veered). v. – change direction suddenly

Friggin Chicken

"Twenty-eight feet, twenty-nine feet, thirty feet," I yelled to the crowd. "Thirty-one feet, thirty-two feet, thirty-three feet, thirty-four feet, thirty-five feet, thirty-six feet." The crowd started to count with me. "Thirty-seven, thirty-eight, thirty-nine, forty"! I began to slow down because I was getting closer to Mrs. Morris'chicken and I placed the tape closer to the floor.

"What's it say?" yelled Dana.
"Yeah, what's it say?" asked another person in the crowd.
"Mrs. Morris chicken went forty-one feet! Mrs. Morris wins!"
"Yea!" shouted all the students from her class.
Emma began to pout and took her place back on the bleachers where she was originally seated. After I finished returning the measuring tape to Mrs. Morris, several students approached me:
"David, can Jack and I play next?"
"No David, let Kate and I go next."
"No David, we want to go next!"
"We want go next go."

"I'm going to make my chicken go 100 million feet."
"Wow David. Your line is getting really long. You better hurry and collect those tickets," Mrs. Morris said with a wink.
She was right. I had at least ten people in line. That was more than Slam Dunk You or any other game going on the gym. The line was so long that Emma had to be my assistant. She helped me collect tickets and measure the distance of chickens. I couldn't believe how many students actually wanted to play Friggin Chicken. Hundreds, thousands, millions! Okay, okay, okay... I'm **exaggerating**, but still way more than I expected.

Beep Hello everyone and good afternoon. The time now is 2:15. We have a few minutes left in our school day so it's time to clean up the games and see which class earned the most money and determine which student is this year's winner. *Beep*

---

exaggerating (ex-ag-ger-at-ing). v. – represent as being larger, greater, better, or worse than it really is

Everyone began to clean up and tally their class and individual ticket count. Dr. Jackson made one final clean up announcement and asked for all classes to report the ticket count. After everyone cleaned up their stations and reported how many tickets they earned, each class had a seat on the bleachers. Every teacher handed a piece a paper with the overall ticket count of the class and each student's individual number count and turned it into Dr. Jackson. He began to add all the scores to determine who this year's winners were.

"Everyone have a seat and be quiet, I'm getting ready to announce who are this year's winners. In 3rd place, the overall winning team is the fantastic first graders; 2nd place for the overall winning team is our fantanbulous fourth graders; and in 1st place the winner of this year's Fall Festival is our stupendous seconder graders." All of the second graders cheered which was so lame because only the best class wins the trip to Great America and the best game wins the homework pass and student of the month.

"Now, let's get to the part that everyone's been waiting on: the individual class winner and the number 1 game at this year's Fall Festivals. In 3rd place for best individual class is Mrs. Hutchinson's 1st grade class."

Everyone in the gym applauded Mrs. Hutchinson's class for winning.

"In second place, best individual class is Mr. Bagly's 5th grade class. Well done students," said Dr. Jackson.
Everyone applauded Mr. Bagly's class just as they applauded Mrs. Hutchinson.

"Can I have a drum roll, please?" asked Dr. Jackson. All students, teachers, and parents in the gym stomped their feet filling the gym with a loud roaring drumroll sensation.

"And this year's individual class first place winner is Mrs. Moorrrrrrrrrrreeeee's 2nd grade class!"

Oh no! I was for sure that Dr. Jackson was going to say Mrs. Morris' class was the winning team. After all we had Slam Dunk You-that game always has lots of tickets.

Everyone in the gym was moaning and groaning because they didn't win. Especially my class; we thought for sure we had won this year.

"Quiet everyone I have one last announcement for this year's best game host winner."

"In third place we have Lauren Adams with 652 tickets. In second place with 702 tickets is Colby Kimble. And for first place of this year's Fall Festival- drum roll please- we have a three way tie! With 816 tickets: Jayden O'Neil, Michael Hunter, and David Allen. Let's give these guys a hand clap for their amazing game s and creative effort."

No way! Me! I won best game, and I'm tied with Michael Hunter and Jayden O'Neil. How in the world did Friggin Chicken ever raise that many tickets anyway? This is amazing!
Dr. Jackson rudely interrupted my thoughts, "As you all know there can only be one winner, so can we have all three game show hosts come down."

We all got up and stood by Dr. Jackson in the middle of the gym. "Since we have a tie, I am going to let you, the audience, decide who this year's winner will be. When I say each person's name, then I want you guys to make as much noise as you possibly can for the person you want to win."

This is sure to be a big waste of my time. Even though Friggin Chicken tied with two other games the entire school thinks I'm a dork and would never vote for me. I should just sit down and save myself some embarrassment.

"First up *(again, Dr. Jackson is interrupting my thoughts)* is Michael Hunter. Come on guys give it up for Michael Hunter." It sounded as if every single person in the gym was screaming, clapping, stomping on the bleachers; making any noise as loud as they could. Dr. Jackson waved his hand in the air to settle everyone down.

"Alright that was a mighty roar for Mr. Hunter. Now let's see if Jayden O'Neil can beat that. Everybody give it up for Jayden".
"Yea!" yelled everyone in his class. He got a few other claps, but it didn't sound anywhere nearly as loud as Michael Hunter's.
Again, Dr. Jackson waved his hand to stop the cheers and the claps.
"That was quite some cheering, but it was not quite as loud as Michael's. I'm sorry, but please go have a seat."
As Jayden walked to his seat, I began to sweat. My arm pits were sweaty, my forehead was sweaty, even my hands were sweaty.
I knew the only people that were going to clap for me were my mom, dad, Aaden, and Mrs. Morris. Emma will not want anyone to even know she was related to me.
"Alright everyone, give it up"…

"For cheesehead," shouted someone from the bleachers.
All the students were laughing at me. I lowered my head in shame and began walking back to my seat.
Dr. Jackson grabbed my hand and forced me to stay put. He used his other hand to silence the heckling and laughing.

"Students at this school know better than to pick on other students. I want the name of the person who shouted cheesehead and if anyone else blurts out an inappropriate comment, then you will have detention and silent lunch for the remainder of the school year. So let's try this again. Let's give it up for David Allen!"

To my surprise, the gym filled with the same roar it did for Michael

Hunter. Some students were stomping on the bleachers. Others were cheering and screaming to the top of their lungs. I can't believe it. They actually liked my game.

Dr. Jackson raised his hand to quiet the screams.

"Whoa! That was so loud I thought my ears were going to pop! Unfortunately, Dublin Elementary, we still don't have a winner. It appears Michael and David are tied for first place. I need you guys to give it up one more time for whoever you think should be this year's winner."

As Dr. Jackson was speaking, some of the students started chanting, "David, David, David, David," before Dr. Jackson even said my name. Before long, it seems as if everyone in the gym was saying my name.

I'm wondering what has gotten into everyone. Is this a joke? Were people really cheering for me, King David?
Again, he motioned for everyone to be silent. "Okay, let's give a hand clap for Michael Hunter." There was a loud wave of claps that filled the gymnasium. After the cheers stopped, Dr. Jackson said, "Let's give a hand clap for"…

"David, David, David, David."

Everyone was chanting my name again. They were stomping on the bleachers, screaming, and some students were even standing. This has got to be some sort of dream. There's no way the school's cheese head could possibly be getting this kind of **recognition**, but apparently I was.

Dr. Jackson motioned for everyone to be silent, but everyone continued screaming and clapping. So, over the loud noise Dr. Jackson

---

recognition (rec-og-ni-tion). n. – the action or process of recognizing or being recognized, in particular
baffled (baf-fled). v. – totally bewilder or perplex

announced me as this year's Fall Festival winner!
Yes, I thought to myself. No homework for a week, but I still can't help but wonder why I got so many cheers, and how did I ever beat one of the most popular kids in school. I'm **baffled**.

Dr. Jackson handed me my trophy and I ran over to where my parents were standing. Mom gave me a big hug and said, "I knew you could do it. All you had to do was make the game your own." "Yes son. This reminds me of when I won the Pine Derby. It was 19"…

"Oh no! Not the Pine Derby story again!" I shouted.
"Come on guys let's go home and celebrate your brother's victory," said mom.

As we were leaving out, several students congratulated me and gave me high-fives; students I didn't even know knew I existed. I overheard a few students saying how fast they got their chickens to go. Others were saying how cool the game was, especially when the chickens would drift. I couldn't believe people really thought Friggin Chicken was a good game.

As we were getting in the car, I saw Michael Hunter. We made eye contact and he mouthed, "This isn't over dweeb."

I didn't know what to say back to him. For the first time, I was speechless. I was so happy that I won that I didn't have one mean thing to say, but I did imagine me pounding him for calling me a dweeb.

"Come on David, get in the car" said Emma. "Let's go celebrate." Just as we were about to drive away, Mrs. Morris stopped us. "David, can I speak with you alone, please?"

I looked at my mom and dad and slowly got out of the car. "Yes, Mrs. Morris. Did I do something wrong? I didn't cheat, I promise!

I added the wheels and feathers by myself."

"No David, you're not in trouble. I just wanted you to know that I am extremely proud of you and I also want to say that I told you so! I told you if you were creative and made the game yours, then you could win! Now go on and have fun with your family."

I gave Mrs. Morris a big hug because she was right. I did win, and I plan on winning every year from now on. As for Michael Hunter, this is only the beginning of me winning against him!